ROB ROY LIBRARY

No. 3

1ᵈ

THE BLACK CAPTAIN

"Like lightning the Black Captain thrust at Rob Roy's throat, but the Highland Chieftain leapt to one side, and with one terrible sweep of his claymore hurled the Black Captain over the precipice."

POCKET BUDGET LIBRARY

NOW ON SALE,

GRAND COMPLETE STORIES

IN ATTRACTIVE ILLUSTRATED COLOURED COVERS.

1. SONS OF THE WAVES. A Stirring Story of Fighting at Sea.
2. JACK MARLIN'S SCHOOLDAYS. A Story of Rattling Fun and Adventures at School.
3. WITH THE FUSILIERS; Or, Brothers in Arms. An Exciting Soldier Story.
4. BELTRANO THE NAMELESS; Or, The Cavaliers of Castile. A Grand Old-Time Tale of the Days of Chivalry.
5. THE PIKEMEN OF SEDGEMOOR. The Story of the Daring Adventures of Dick Seymour.
6. MIDSHIPMAN JACK MARLIN. A Splendid Story of Adventure at Sea.
7. IN THE RANKS. A Rattling Story of Adventure in India
8. ULLAM THE UNKNOWN. A Stirring Story of the Scottish Wars.
9. LOYAL TO THE KING. A Grand Story of Remarkable Adventure.
10. DICK ASHTON OF CRANWORTH. A Rattling School Story.
11. ON THE SPANISH MAIN. Jack Marlin's Further Adventures at Sea
12. SWORD AND CROSSBOW; Or, The Rightful Heir of Battleden.
13. WHO SERVES THE KING? A Stirring Story of Adventure in the Days of King Charles.
14. THE GRAMMAR SCHOOL BRIGADE; Or, The Rattling Adventures of Eight Schoolboys.
15. AFLOAT AND ASHORE. The Further Exciting Adventures of Lieutenant Jack Marlin.
16. THE GOLDEN KNIGHT; Or, The Secret of the Crown of Iona.

EACH BOOK CONTAINS A LONG COMPLETE STORY OF ABOUT 38,000 WORDS.

Each Number Price ONE PENNY; by Post, 1½d.

FOUR SPLENDID NEW NUMBERS READY ON NOV. 26.

IN HIGHLY ATTRACTIVE PICTORIAL COVERS PRINTED IN COLOURS.

17. THE BOYS OF REDMINSTER. A School Story full of Fun and Adventures.
18. CAPTAIN JACK MARLIN. His Adventures in the Four Quarters of the Globe.
19. RUPERT THE YOUNG SWORDSMAN A Grand Old-Time Story.
20. FIGHTING JACK. A Thrilling Soldier Story.

PLEASE ORDER AT ONCE FROM YOUR NEWSAGENT.

London: JAMES HENDERSON & SONS, Red Lion House, Red Lion Court, Fleet Street, E.C.

THE BLACK CAPTAIN

By ANGUS MACLEAN.

CHAPTER I.

KIDNAPPED.

"ALASTAIR!" shouted Rob Roy, as he peered from his cave that overlooked the magnificent Loch Ard. "Alastair! What means this in the lands of the MacGregor?"

Alastair uttered an ejaculation of surprise as, reaching Rob Roy's side, he saw a young boy running for dear life on the roadway that skirted the lake.

"By heaven!" shouted Rob Roy, as he caught a glimpse of the boy's pursuer. "The Black Captain!"

Even in the distance the swarthy face of the pursuer could be seen, showing all its malignant features.

"How came that villain and robber here?" muttered Rob Roy. "Quick, Alastair, let us to the boy's rescue!"

In a moment Rob Roy and Alastair swung themselves over the rocky edge of the cave and, quickly descending the rope that dangled over the precipice, gained the roadway.

In the distance they could see a flaxen-haired lad of about twelve years of age running like the wind, but his grim pursuer was close upon him.

"By Coilantogle," shouted Rob Roy, as he and Alastair raced side by side. "He has caught the child. Onward, Alastair, onward!"

Like a couple of mountain deer the giant Highland chieftain and his brother rushed down the slopes of the mountain at the foot of which they could see the lad struggling with his dark-featured enemy.

"Help! Help! Help!"

They could hear his cries, but almost immediately, and to their intense amazement, the cries ceased, and both boy and pursuer vanished as if in thin air.

"By all that is holy!" exclaimed Alastair, crossing himself, as he drew up, breathless, on the spot where they had seen the boy. "Mystery follows on mystery: where have they got to?"

"Somewhere," muttered Rob Roy, "that is certain. But this is most exasperating."

"He is possessed of the Evil One, I have heard," replied Alastair.

"Fudge, Alastair, fudge! The man they call the Black Captain—and that was he we saw—is a scoundrel, and a clever scoundrel, too. It bodes no good to have him here."

"No," responded Alastair, "he bodes no good. And if he has the broken men of the north behind him, then heaven help us."

As they spoke they saw another figure running wildly towards them. He was a middle-aged man, with terror depicted on his face.

"Oh, good sirs," he panted, "I am undone. The boy, where is he?"

"That is more than I can say, good man," replied Rob Roy, kindly; "but who is he?"

"The heir to Craigfillan."

It was now Rob Roy's turn to look aghast.

"The heir to Craigfillan!" he exclaimed, starting back in surprise. "Why, I saw him in his father's castle but a fortnight ago."

"Then, sir, you are Rob Roy?"

"I am," replied the Highland chieftain.

"Very well, sir," responded the man, "I am one of his father's retainers, and since your last visit, Alan, that is the boy's name, has talked of nothing else but Rob Roy and his cave."

"Poor little lad!" ejaculated Rob Roy. "I promised to take him there one day."

"But he would not wait," said the retainer. "He would start off, and while I made the boat fast at the moorings he wandered into the woods. Suddenly I heard his cry for help, but no one could I see."

"Listen to me," interrupted Rob Roy; "he has been kidnapped. In the distance I recognised the figure of the monster called the Black Captain."

The man shivered.

"The Black Captain," he shuddered. "I have heard some fearful tales of him."

"Who has not?" replied Alastair. "Why, only six months ago he and his band of robbers laid waste the country from Applecross to Athol."

"And," said Rob Roy, "he has ravaged the lands of the low country, and I have heard he has a stronghold amongst the Cheviot Hills, and also a place of refuge in distant Kirkcudbright, among the moss-hags of the border."

"He is a fiend incarnate. But the boy," exclaimed the retainer; "has he been stolen for the sake of reward?"

Rob Roy did not answer at once.

"Let us hope so," he replied at length, and very thoughtfully. "Let us hope so; but there is a mystery attached to the scoundrel and the Laird of Craigfillan. Let us hope it is but for reward."

"Let us be up and doing. The villain cannot have left the glen," said Alastair.

Rob Roy seemed lost in thought.

"I can remember my father telling me that his father told him of the presence of a secret passage in this very glen, but I have never seen it. Still, it must be here, and that scoundrel knows it. Come, let us search. While I was a lad I searched in vain, and believed that the passage was but a myth."

High and low they searched, but no passage could they find. Where they fancied they had seen the boy disappear was merely a waste of broken rock and bracken. They left no stone unturned, but no trace of the missing ones could they find.

"Let us return to the cave," said Rob Roy, "and although I am again an outlaw, I shall never sleep twice on the same spot or eat twice in the same place until I have restored young Alan to his gallant father."

CHAPTER II.
THE PURSUIT.

Rob Roy, accompanied by Alastair and the retainer, arrived at the foot of a precipitous rock on the face of which one of his caves was built.

Whistling sharply three times, Rob Roy looked upwards.

Immediately a long rope ladder was lowered over the cliff.

"Ascend first," said Rob Roy to the retainer, "Alastair and I will follow."

In a short space of time they gained the entrance to the cave. It was but a narrow hole and was hidden from view by a natural balustrade of limestone that formed part of the face of the cliff.

Immediately above their heads was a large and gnarled oak tree that grew out of the scarred rocks.

"In time of trouble," said Rob Roy, pointing upwards to the tree, "we can drop from the top of the cliff to the tree and thus evade pursuers. But let us enter."

"Go feet first," said Rob Roy, "and thus prevent accident. If by chance the rock became loose you would be held a prisoner with no chance of escape."

"Wait," exclaimed Rob Roy, as the retainer disappeared, "wait when you get through."

In a moment Rob Roy and Alastair passed through the narrow entrance.

Rob Roy at once lighted a torch, while the retainer gazed about in wonder. The cavern widened from the entrance and the walls glittered with Highland claymores and brass-studded shields.

"Welcome," said Rob Roy, "to the home of the MacGregor," as he swept his hand towards the glittering weapons. "This is but the storehouse of the clan."

As they proceeded, the ruddy light of the torch was reflected on the face of a large expanse of silent water, and as the retainer peered into the blackness beyond, he observed a boat moored to the wall of the cavern.

The boat was a curiously shaped affair. It was flat bottomed and very broad.

Motioning the retainer to get into the

boat, Rob Roy ordered him to lie down flat, Alastair at the same time following suit.

Seizing an oar in his powerful right hand, and holding aloft the torch in his left, Rob Roy, with one powerful sweep, sent the boat skimming along the placid surface of the water.

Soon a trickling of water was heard, and immediately Rob Roy placed himself flat in the boat but still holding the torch.

In a moment they were carried by a current through a narrow gorge, so narrow, indeed, that the torch overhead scraped the rugged stones, and soon they emerged into a blaze of light.

They were now in a cavern of immense size, and well-lighted with lamps and fir-torches that were fixed in iron holders round the walls.

As the boat grated on the shore of the inland lake, the retainer saw a huge table in the centre of the cave laden with deer's flesh and large triangular pieces of oat cake, while beside the table sat a sweet-faced woman spinning flax with a distaff and old oaken spinning machine.

This was Mary MacGregor, the chieftainess of the clan.

She rose at once and embraced her husband as he jumped on shore.

"Mary," he said, "I come but to leave you. The young heir of Craigfillan has been captured by the Black Captain."

"Heaven have mercy on us, Rob," she cried, "when that evil man is about. What brought him here?"

"I know not, save that he had followed the young heir, but to beard the Mac-Gregor in his own lands and disappear as if by magic is an offence not lightly to be overlooked."

"He will carry the boy to the bleak mosses of Kirkcudbright and murder him."

"What makes you think so, Mary?"

"He has his stronghold there; at least, so it is said, and evidently he has a purpose in taking the young heir. It bodes no good. My gallant husband, speed you to the rescue. Never let it be said that Mary MacGregor stood in the path of duty of her husband."

And so saying, she went to the wall of the cavern and, taking a brass-studded shield of bull-hide, placed it on her husband's left arm.

"And I go with you," said Alastair.

"No, good Alastair," returned Rob Roy. "I will pursue the scoundrel alone.

If I return not in ten days from now, bring the clansmen to the border and scour the place for the missing heir."

"Go," continued Rob Roy, "to the Laird of Craigfillan and tell him that I have gone in pursuit. Let him also send his men in search. I am to make for the wilds of Kirkcudbright for, if report be true, it is there this mysterious Black Captain has his haunt."

In a moment Rob Roy boarded the boat and was soon lost to view.

CHAPTER III.

ENTRAPPED.

For two days Rob Roy journeyed southwards. Swinging along, the young giant, in kilt and plaid, with claymore, dirk, and targe, covered the distance in an incredibly short time.

As he strode along the bleak moors of Kirkcudbright—lonesome, bleak lands, the scene of many murders and rapine—his attention was attracted by the screams of a woman proceeding from the edge of an adjoining wood.

Rapidly making to where the sounds came from, he discovered a woman bound hand and foot and pinned to the ground by her long, raven hair. So closely was her hair pegged to the ground that she could not move her head one inch.

"What means this, lady?" exclaimed Rob Roy, advancing.

"Save me, save me!" she cried. "Some wicked robbers have carried off my husband and have left me bound here. Undo my hair, undo my hair. It pains me greatly."

Rob Roy knelt down, undid her bonds, and tenderly pulled the pegs up that bound the woman's tresses to the ground.

Suddenly Rob Roy looked up. Six armed men—ferocious-looking bandits—were close on him.

In a second he turned to spring to his feet, but ere he could do so the woman pinned his arms from behind and pulled him backwards.

Before he could recover, one of the ruffians sprang upon him and dealt him a fearful blow on the head with a bludgeon.

With a superhuman effort, Rob Roy sprang to his feet, but the woman clung to his sword, while another ruffian struck him on the head.

In a moment he was overpowered, and

the ruffians, taking a rope from the treacherous woman, securely bound him.

"Take him to the dungeon of the eastern bastion," ordered a gruff voice.

Glancing upwards at the speaker, Rob Roy saw that he was the prisoner of the Black Captain.

"You scoundrel!" shouted Rob Roy. "What mean you by your villainy?"

"Have a care," snarled the Black Captain, his dark features becoming demon-like with passion, "have a care, or I shall despatch you where you lie."

"My hands are tied," returned Rob Roy, boldly, "but my tongue is free, and I tell you to your face, you villain, that you will repent this day's work."

"Carry him away—away to the dungeon with him!" shouted the Black Captain.

The robbers lifted the Highland chieftain on their shoulders and marched off.

For some time they tramped over the moors, and no sign of a castle could Rob Roy see. But he had time to observe his captors fully.

They were all stalwart men, rough and powerful, with coarse faces, and dressed like the ordinary moss-troopers as these border robbers were called. They carried swords and knives, and although at present no horses were near, they wore spurs—cruel-looking rowels of very large make. Their clothing was of rough home-spun material.

Their leader, the Black Captain, strode on in front. He was also armed with sword and dagger which hung from a belt of horse-hair that drew his roughly-fitting fustian jacket together. His beard was long and black, in perfect keeping with his raven hair, while his skin, as much as could be seen on his hairy face, was almost as dark as a negro's.

On his head he wore a curious-looking helm of iron, shaped like the helmet of the ancient Greeks. But the most remarkable thing about him was his face. It was cruel and malignant, without a single trace of love or pity in it.

The moss-troopers now began to feel the weight of their burden, particularly when they began to ascend some rising ground.

"Unbind his legs and let him walk," grunted the Black Captain, scowling.

Rob Roy was lowered to the ground and his legs unbound. The dauntless Highland chieftain looked about him for a means of escape, but he suddenly recollected that his hands were tied. There was nothing for it but to wait.

"My pretty prisoner!" sneered the Black Captain, "your doom is sure, so needless it is for you to attempt escape. If you move one foot from your escort I shall cut you down." And the Black Captain drew his sword viciously.

When they had reached the top of the rising ground Rob Roy, much to his surprise, saw in front of him a strongly fortified castle, built in the hollow of the hill and cunningly hidden from the flat surrounding country by the rising ground around it.

A moat ran round it, and in a few minutes they were tramping over the drawbridge.

Rob Roy was carefully led over the courtyard and conducted down to the dungeon. As the heavy door clanged behind him he was left in utter darkness.

CHAPTER IV.

IN CRAIGFILLAN CASTLE.

When the Laird of Craigfillan heard that the Black Captain had kidnapped his son he was struck dumb with consternation.

"It means murder, pure and simple," he managed to gasp after a little time. "Murder pure and simple!"

"Murder!" echoed Alastair, who brought the news to him.

"Yes, murder. You know not the Black Captain."

"Nothing to his good."

"That were impossible. Listen to me. That man has been the bug-bear of my existence. I have but one son, and I have had to guard him jealously lest he should fall into the hands of the Black Captain."

"Why so, why is that?"

"Because," came the unexpected answer, "the Black Captain is the heir to the estates were my boy dead."

"Then," said Alastair, "there is no time to be lost if we are to rescue him alive."

"Not a moment," exclaimed the Laird. "Ho there, call the retainers together. We must scour the border for the villain."

A strong party forthwith set out with the Laird at their head and took the direction of the wild bleak moors of the moss-troopers.

CHAPTER V.

In the Robbers' Stronghold.

Imprisonment ill-suited the Highland chieftain, but the thought that troubled him was not his own escape but the finding of the lost heir. While several plans passed through his active brain, the door of his prison grated on its hinges and a moss-trooper stood in the doorway.

Before the robber could open the door, Rob Roy sprung behind it and stood motionless.

"Ho! there!" shouted the moss-trooper. "Ho! there! Advance to the doorway, your presence is required before the chief."

Rob Roy dared scarcely to breathe, so stock-still did he stand. He had a plan in his head.

"Ho! there! prisoner, advance to to the doorway." Again exclaimed the robber, himself advancing and peering into the dungeon. "Ho! there!"

The robber, confident that the bound prisoner was practically defenceless, now boldly stepped into the dungeon.

Immediately he crossed the threshold and cleared the doorway, Rob Roy, securely bound as his arms were, sprang upon the man and dealt him such a blow with his head just behind the ear that the robber dropped senseless as if he had been shot.

Rob Roy quickly bent down with his back to his fallen foe, and drawing the knife from the robber's belt, quickly cut his bonds.

In a few minutes Rob Roy dressed himself in the robber's clothes and put his own on the latter.

"Hurry up, there!" called a voice in the passage. "The chief is waiting!"

Fortunately for our hero the passage was dark, save for the light of a feeble lamp at the further end. Rob Roy swiftly advanced. He heard the tramp of feet advancing. There seemed to be no escape.

Half-way along was a crevice, evidently the bricked-up end of an old passage.

Into this crevice Rob Roy darted, and only just in time, for several robbers made their appearance.

"Hurry up, there!" exclaimed their leader, but the words died in his mouth when he saw the open door and no reply was given.

"This is strange," said the man. "The prisoner has fainted. Ho! Jamie Johnston, whaur are ye?"

Bending over the supposed Rob Roy the man gave vent to a fearful oath.

"That cursed Highlander has escaped us."

The cry was repeated, and the men rushed along the passage.

Rob Roy crouched in the shadow, but ready to defend himself. However, the robbers were so excited that much caution was hardly necessary.

From his hiding-place Rob Roy heard the turmoil in the robbers' stronghold, and high above the row rose the voice of the Black Captain.

"Search high and low!" he kept shouting. "Recapture him alive or dead."

"Better capture him alive," said another voice. "There is a price upon his head, and we should kill two birds with one stone. Better that the Government should cut off his head, and we pocket the reward."

"You are right," said the Black Captain, "but recapture him in any case. First of all examine the dungeon, then every other part of the castle."

Rob Roy heard the words and grasped his sword firmly. Drawing his cap over his eyes so as to shade his face as much as possible, he resolved on a bold plan.

He would mix with the rabble and endeavour to find the whereabouts of the young heir.

As the crowd rushed along to the dungeon, Rob Roy left his place of concealment and joined the throng.

"He is not here, that is a certainty."

"That is so, Harry of Auchentroid," replied another voice.

"Make way there!" shouted the Black Captain, advancing. "Make way there!"

As soon as the Black Captain had entered the dungeon, Rob Roy sprang outside and shut the door with a clang and instantly shot the bolt on the outside.

"Ha! ha! ha!" exclaimed Rob Roy, "my pretty prisoners. A nice crew I have got now for the hangman's rope."

A volley of curses was the only response.

Then above the din again rose the voice of the Black Captain.

"Beware, Rob Roy!" he shouted. "Be not too premature. My turn will come!"

"Yes!" exclaimed Rob Roy. "Your turn of the rope will be first."

Making certain that the bolt was secure, Rob Roy ran along the passage and into the main corridor.

"Alan Craigfillan! Alan Craigfillan!" he shouted. "Be not afraid, Rob Roy is coming to your rescue. Alan Craigfillan!"

There was no reply.

Passing into another passage Rob Roy kept shouting the young lad's name, and was rewarded by hearing a muffled sound at the further end.

Quickly passing along, Rob Roy discovered a number of cells, and by shouting at the door of each found the one in which young Alan was confined.

In a second he undid the bolt.

"Alan, Alan, my boy! Are you well?"

"Oh! Rob Roy!" exclaimed Alan, in delight. "I am so glad you have come. I was told I should die to-night. I am hungry."

"Quick!" exclaimed Rob Roy, "we have no time to lose. That treacherous woman may hear us."

"What woman?"

"Never mind, my boy. I'll tell you later on. Quick!"

Seizing the boy by the hand Rob Roy hastened from the cell and ran along the main corridor.

"This way for the drawbridge," he whispered. "Let the chains go. Never mind the noise."

The drawbridge fell with a thunderous clap.

"Now," exclaimed Rob Roy, leading Alan over the bridge, "let anyone cross our path and woe betide him!"

CHAPTER VI.

THE ESCAPE.

The night was dark, but Rob Roy guided his path over the bleak moor by the stars. Gaining the top of the ridge that concealed the robbers' stronghold, he struck a northerly direction.

"Alan, my boy, you are tired. Let me carry you," and Rob Roy hoisted Alan on his broad back as if the boy was but a feather-weight.

"Keep your ears open," whispered Rob Roy, "for we are in a dangerous country and know not who are friends and who are enemies."

Rob Roy strode proudly onwards.

"I see a light," exclaimed Alan.

"Where about?" asked Rob Roy. "It may only be a will-of-the-wisp."

"A dead candle," said the boy, below his breath.

"That is but superstition, my boy," returned Rob Roy. "The dead candle is but a phosphorescent light coming from the decayed matter in the bog, and people say that it is a warning—that it portends death and shows the way beforehand the funeral is to take."

"I still see the light," said Alan.

"Ah!" laughed Rob Roy, good-humouredly, "you are taller than I; but where away, my boy?"

"Right in front."

"You are right!" exclaimed Rob Roy. "It has just come into view."

Standing still for a moment, Rob Roy strained his eyes at the light. Then stepping backwards a few paces he said: "It is a stationary light—the light of a cottage which lies below us. We are on a rising eminence. From the other side I could not see it. Now, let me think."

"If it is a cottage light, we may get shelter for the night."

"Yes," mused Rob Roy, "but we must be very careful. The cottage may belong to a Border crofter, but more than likely to a moss hag or Border raider. With the raiders we are safe, but with some of the Border cut-throats we had better give them elbow-room."

"I feel very cold and tired," said Alan.

Rob Roy did not answer for a minute.

"Well," he said at last, "we must take our chance. It may be all right."

As Rob Roy marched on over the gorse the light became more and more distinct, until a small cottage loomed in view.

Walking boldly to the doorway, Rob Roy knocked loudly.

Instantly there was a scuffling of feet, and a gruff voice demanded, "Who's there?"

"Travellers from Carlisle, who want a night's shelter from wind and rain."

"What want ye in this part from Carlisle?"

"Visiting the High Steward of Kirk-cudbright."

"How many are there?" asked the voice, suspiciously.

"Two—a man and a boy."

During the conversation there had been much scuffling of feet, and after a lot of muttering a man flung the door open.

He was a coarse-looking man with beetling eyebrows, and he scrutinised his visitors sharply as the flood of light from the doorway fell on the giant figure of Rob Roy with the flaxen-haired Alan perched on his broad shoulders.

"You are welcome to my humble cot," said the man, with a futile attempt at geniality; "you do not belong to this part."

"No," replied Rob Roy; "I belong to the North, and for what we have we pay."

A curious leer came into the man's eyes.

"You are welcome for your own sake. I am a poor man and you may have the share of my bread and cheese."

"You keep a clean house," replied Rob Roy, casually, as he deposited Alan in an old-fashioned chair by the fireside and nodded towards the sand freshly strewn on the floor.

The man started.

"I have but myself, and the only time I have to clean the place is before I go to bed. But I often have visitors. Indeed, I put up strangers that have lost their way very often."

"We have not lost our way, but should be very glad of a rest for the night."

"You are welcome. The visitors' room, as I call it, is ready for you whenever you like."

"I think," said Rob Roy, "we had better have some bread and cheese first."

"Yes," chimed in Alan, "I feel hungry."

"We'll soon settle that," said the man, disappearing to the next room.

As soon as he had gone Rob Roy, unknown to Alan, drew his foot along the sanded floor. A dark, wet stain instantly revealed itself.

"Blood!" muttered Rob Roy. "It is as I thought. There has been murder here! We are in a trap!"

CHAPTER VII.

AT CLOSE QUARTERS.

When the man returned with a wooden platter containing bread and cheese and a pitcher of water, Rob Roy could scarcely keep his hands off the villain. Had he been by himself he would have cut the man down where he stood, but Alan was with him, and any sign of suspicion would bring the hornets down on them both.

"We are much obliged," said Rob Roy, after they had partaken of the bread and cheese. "Now I think a slight rest would do us good."

"I have but the one spare bed," said the man. "Perhaps the boy might have that and you could sleep on the chair by the ingle-neuk."

Not for worlds would Rob Roy have been separated from Alan.

"No," he said, "the one bed will do for both. We are not at all particular, and as I like a long lie in the morning, I do not care for the chair."

"As you please," replied the man, "you are certainly sure of a long lie in the bed. This way."

The man led them across the room and, ushering them through a narrow doorway, bade them once more make themselves at home.

There was nothing peculiar about the bed or bedroom, and Rob Roy examined them both critically. Crawling on the bed, Rob Roy felt down the walls for any concealed door through which an assassin could murder the unsuspecting traveller in his sleep.

"What do you do that for?" asked Alan.

"Hush!" whispered Rob Roy, "this is a peculiar house. No, do not take off your clothes. Lie on the top of the bed. Now try to get a sleep. I will watch awhile."

Meanwhile Rob Roy had closed the door, and placed a chair against it. The door had no lock.

Very soon Alan fell into a deep sleep, but the ears of the Highland chieftain were on the alert.

Sword in hand he sat on the edge of the bed, and he fancied at times he could hear whispering in the adjoining room.

A couple of hours had passed, when an unaccountable feeling of danger possessed him. Something seemed to be impending, and as he glanced at the walls his eyes caught a sight above him that froze his soul with horror.

Slowly, silently, without the slightest noise, the part of the roof above the bed, shaped in the form of a huge lid, was descending on them.

A glance showed that when down this huge iron lid fitted the framework of the bed, and the victim would die of suffocation.

Only a second was to spare. The death-trap almost touched his head. With one spring he drew the boy from below, and as he began to shout through fright Roy Roy held his hand gently over his mouth.

Silently the death-trap enveloped the bed as Rob Roy and Alan stood spellbound for the moment.

"My boy," whispered Rob Roy, "they mean to murder us. This is one of the houses of the Black Captain, where he lures travellers and others to their doom. Take my dirk. We must watch here till morning. And whatever happens, stand behind me, but do not cling to me. I will protect you."

"Hush," repeated Rob Roy, as a movement was heard in the other room.

Rob Roy had put out the light.

"They take it quietly," said a voice that Rob Roy recognised as that of their villainous host. "The big fellow wanted a long lie in the morning, and by St. Andrew, he's getting it."

"Is it time to take off the night-cap?" asked another voice, with hoarse jocularity.

"No, not yet. The fresh air might revive them and we might have a fight for it like last night."

"Well, well, plenty of time."

In the dark bedroom Rob Roy waited holding Alan's hand. For himself the noble Highland chieftain cared not a straw, but for Alan's sake he was content to play a waiting game.

The voices now grew bolder.

"Let us lift the lid," said the voice of the second man. "I will turn the crank and hoist it up, and you can crack their skulls."

"The inhuman wretches," muttered Rob Roy to himself. "Soon I shall make them pay toll for their villainy."

"Go on," said the first man.

Rob Roy darted towards the door and removed the chair and returned with Alan to a corner of the room.

In a minute the man appeared at the door, holding a light above his head.

"Dead as a doornail," he said, as the death-trap began to ascend. "The river Ken will ken them soon."

"Not so dead as you," thundered Rob Roy.

The man dropped the light in fright, and the next moment he fell prone to the ground from a swinging blow from Rob Roy's sword.

The second man ran forward on hearing the noise, and immediately Rob Roy pursued him to the other room.

It was now daylight, as Rob Roy could see by the kitchen windows.

The man ran to the wall and drew out an iron rod. At once Rob Roy felt the floor collapse where he stood, but not before, with a desperate grab, he managed to catch the coat tails of the villain.

In a second, Rob Roy, dragging the man with him, disappeared through the trap door, and splashed into a flowing river.

Rob Roy was a magnificent swimmer and, guessing that the water he was now in was a subterranean tributary of the river Ken, kept his head above water and allowed himself to drift with the current.

In the terrible darkness it was an awful experience, but Rob Roy's brave heart never quailed once.

After what seemed to be an interminable time, but what in reality was but a few minutes, Rob Roy emerged through a cavern-like entrance to the bosom of the river. A few strokes and he reached the shore.

"Now for that villain," muttered Rob Roy, as he watched the entrance of the subterranean river closely.

"Ah!" he ejaculated, as the man's body floated past, "he has gone to his long account."

"Now," said Rob Roy, "to see after Alan."

Rob Roy climbed the river-bank and discovered that the hut was some five hundred yards away, with nothing round it but a wild, bleak moor.

He lost no time in gaining the hut.

"Alan! Alan!" he shouted.

"Yes, yes!" came the answer. "Is that you, Rob Roy? I thought you were dead."

"Are you safe?"

"Yes; but I cannot get out."

"Wait a moment," said Rob Roy, as he approached the doorway, "and we shall see."

"Take care! Take care!" shouted Alan, from the interior. "There is a yawning trapdoor at the entrance."

Rob Roy opened the door cautiously and saw the silent river running below—

the silent river that held secrets never to be revealed until the last day.

"Come along, now," said Rob Roy, seizing a plank at the doorway and bridging the trapdoor. "Let us go from this house of infamy."

"But where is your sword?"

"In the river, my boy."

"Then we are defenceless," said Alan.

"You are," said a voice, "and you are once more my prisoners."

The Black Captain, scowling with hate, stood before them, and behind him were twenty men armed to the teeth.

Flight was useless, and resistance was out of the question.

"Will you go quietly, or will we chop you down where ye are?"

"We are in your power, you villain, but as sure as truth and justice doth prevail, you shall pay for your evil deeds."

"Cease your prating," shrieked the Black Captain, stamping his feet—"cease your prating, or by St. Galloway, you shall not grace our torture chamber."

"Avaunt," replied the dauntless Rob Roy. "Do your worst, you moss-lags and robbers. We are ready."

The Black Captain's men instantly surrounded the prisoners, and marched off towards the stronghold of the robbers.

CHAPTER VIII.

THE ESCAPE.

As the party crossed the moor, Rob Roy pricked up his ears.

In the distance he heard the scream of the Highland curlew. Again the scream—a shrill, piping, piercing whistle—was repeated. Rob Roy listened intently and gazed at the faces of his captors. The scream of the bird was far too common to attract their attention, but they had not heard what Rob Roy had.

A third time the call was repeated with a long, shrill trill.

Instantly Rob Roy, to the amazement of his captors, raised his head and gave vent to a peculiar cry, repeated rapidly three times. At the same instant, before they could recover their surprise, he seized Alan by the body and broke from their midst.

In a moment he was fleeing, with the swiftness of the wind, towards the place from whence the cries had proceeded.

It was now unnecessary for the robbers to ask themselves questions, for there, on their own moors, they saw a sight calculated to make their stony hearts quail.

The sun had burst from behind the dark morning clouds and shone resplendent on a line of leaping figures, dressed in the red tartan of the MacGregor, with flashing claymores and glinting brass-studded shields.

The Black Captain saw at a glance that the vengeance of the MacGregor was at hand.

"Ard Choile! Ard Choile! Grigalach! Grigalach!"

A wild cheer rose as Alastair, bounding forward, shook his brother by the hand. But there was no time to wait.

"To the hut, to the hut!" shouted the Black Captain.

Not a moment too soon were they. In a twinkling the MacGregors surrounded the place.

"Give me a claymore," said Rob Roy. "Follow me and be careful."

The yawning trapdoor still stood there, but not a sign of the Black Captain or his men was to be seen. The three rooms of the house and every nook and cranny were carefully examined, but no trace was to be found of them.

"There must be a secret passage from the stronghold to this hut," said Rob Roy. "Set the place on fire."

In a few minutes the hut was a blazing mass of ruins.

As they watched the cottage burning, Rob Roy plied his brother with questions.

"Where is Craigfillan?" he asked.

"He seems to be fated to bad luck," replied Alastair, "for when he started with us he fell from his horse the first day and broke his leg."

"Most unfortunate," replied Rob Roy, "I should have liked to witness the meeting of father and son."

"By the way, he sent a message to you, Rob."

"What was that?"

"That he wished to see you before you took any steps to punish the Black Captain."

"And why should that be?"

"I know not, Rob, but I observed that he was very earnest on that point."

"Well, what do you advise?"

"That we return with the young heir and then decide our plans."

"But I have sworn to clear the country of this monster and his gang, and it shall be so."

"By all means, Rob, but our force

is at present too small. Let us return, send round the fiery cross, but deal with the robbers according to their deserts."

"The advice is good. MacGregors, let us return to the north. When we come here again we shall rid the world of a nuisance."

CHAPTER IX.

THE BLACK CAPTAIN.

"You shall be safe here," said Rob Roy, to Alan, who stood lost in admiration at the cave, or rather caves. "When you want fresh air go to the balustrade in front, and be careful not to show yourself above the heather. In the meantime I will go and see your father."

"A thousand thanks, noble Mac-Gregor," said the Laird of Craigfillan, as Rob Roy entered his presence. "Had I lost my son, I should have broken my heart."

"'Twas but the duty of a man," returned Rob Roy, "and sorry I was that I could not prevent the scoundrel carrying him off. The Black Captain knows the ground."

"He does," replied the Laird, "and it is of him I would speak."

"Say on, Craigfillan, I am all ears."

"The Black Captain, MacGregor, knows the land. I am an older man than you, Rob Roy, and when I tell you that as a boy—long before you were born—I and the Black Captain played by the banks of Loch Ard, you may be surprised."

"I am, Craigfillan, I am. This is the first I have heard of it."

"I have never mentioned it, because it brings back bitter memories. The Black Captain is my brother."

"What!" exclaimed Rob Roy. "I knew there was some connection, but not so near as that."

"Yes, Rob Roy, he is my brother, and he broke his mother's and his father's heart. He held a commission in the army of Louis of France, and for the murder of a comrade had to flee the country. At first he came to the shores of Loch Ard, but knowing that there was no scope for his villainy in the lands of the Macregor, he took up his haunt in the Cheviots somewhere, besides having a stronghold in the wilds of Assynt."

"Reckless and more reckless he be-came, and he has made my life a burden. Again and again he has threatened to kidnap and murder my boy, and has openly boasted to my face that he shall yet be my heir, and yet I should like to wean him from his evil ways, for, after all, he is my brother."

"It is impossible, Craigfillan. I would be the last one to utter a harsh word, but it is impossible. So certain am I of that fact that I have kept your son in my care, and there he shall remain until the Black Captain—brother though he be—and his band are no more."

The old laird bowed his head.

"Perhaps it is best," he murmured, "but it is hard, it is hard."

"One thing I wish to ask," said Rob Roy. "Does the Black Captain know of a secret passage through the mountains."

The Laird of Craigfillan started.

"Ah!" he said, reminiscently, "when I was a boy there was a passage from the valley on the north side of Loch Ard to the other side of the mountain."

"And is the entrance at the bottom of the valley?"

"It is."

"But it is strange that I should not know it."

"It is not strange, Rob Roy, for we boys, I think, were the last that knew of it, and as I fancied, this lost brother of mine might avail himself of it I held my peace."

"It is of little use to him now."

"No, for I am afraid his hour has come. You know what we call Queen Mary's chair?"

"Yes, the rocking chair."

"The very same. Well, that covers the entrance to the secret passage. It rocks backwards and forwards, but a push on it sidewards reveals the secret it covers."

"You surprise me," said Rob Roy.

"Ah!" said the laird, sadly. "Live and learn, MacGregor. I am an older man than you, and I ought to have carried this secret with me."

"It matters not," replied Rob Roy, "for the peace and safety of widows and children shall not be disturbed by marauders."

The laird again bowed his head.

"Adieu," said Rob Roy.

"Adieu," repeated the laird. "Have mercy on him when you meet."

"Such mercy," thought Rob Roy, as

he withdrew, "that he has shown to the needy and oppressed."

CHAPTER X.

THE RECAPTURE.

When Rob Roy left his cave, Alan Craigfillan had every intention of obeying the injunction not to go beyond the balustrade in front of the cave, but the temptation to climb the gnarled tree and thus try to gain the top of the cliff was too great for his spirit of adventure.

For some time he sat enjoying the scene—the beautiful lake below, the towering mountains, the cloud-capped Ben Lomond, the dizzy cliffs over deep Loch Chon—but soon his gaze became fixed on the tree above.

In a very little time he was climbing it, and elated with his success, scrambled on to the ledge by the topmost branches and thence upwards to the top of the cliff.

"So, ho, youngster," said a rough voice.

Alan turned. The Black Captain stood before him.

With a spring forward he seized the boy, and holding his hand over his mouth effectually prevented him from calling out.

"You young spawn!" he shouted, as he gained the entrance to the secret passage. "Here your bones shall lie and rot, and not a soul shall know of it."

With that the Black Captain dragged him along, and coming to an open part of the cavern, lighted a torch.

Quickly he pinioned the boy with a stout rope and secured him firmly to a ring that was suspended from the wall close at hand.

"Stay here and rot, while in years to come, when I have earned a rest, I shall enjoy the lands of Craigfillan."

Alan uttered not a word, for he was afraid that the evil Captain might kill him at once in a fit of passion.

In a minute the Black Captain disappeared muttering maledictions.

CHAPTER XI.

SAVED AGAIN.

When Rob Roy returned from his visit to Craigfillan his first question was of Alan.

"Where is Alan?" he demanded of Alastair; but Alastair did not know.

He had seen him at the cave's mouth not long before.

"Then," exclaimed Rob Roy, fiercely, "he has been kidnapped again. Come, Alastair, to the secret passage."

Before Alastair had time to ask what passage he meant, Rob Roy had scaled the balustrade of the cave and was sliding down the rope.

Alastair followed, and in a short time they arrived at Queen Mary's Chair.

Alastair looked at Rob Roy in surprise, as he pushed the stone vigorously to one side, and immediately it remained suspended at an angle of 45 degrees, while an entrance like a man-hole with steps was exposed to view.

"Follow me," said Rob Roy, "Craigfillan told me about it."

Rob Roy descended the steps, followed by Alastair, when the stone suddenly rolled back in its place, leaving them in total darkness.

"The scoundrel may have brought the boy here," said Rob Roy.

"Alan! Alan!" he shouted; but only the vaulted cavern returned the echoes.

They pushed forward in the darkness.

"Alan! Alan!" again shouted Rob Roy. This time a faint cry came in response.

"Forward!" cried Alastair. "That is Alan's voice."

"Alan! Alan!" again rang through the cavern.

"I am here. I am here!" shouted Alan.

"Where?"

"Here. Bound to the wall. There are some torches near."

"Alastair," said Rob Roy, "your flint and your fleurish. Strike a light."

Alastair struck vigorously with his "fleurish"—a band of steel covering his knuckles—on a piece of flint. The spark soon caught a piece of touch paper which, under Alastair's powerful lungs, quickly fanned itself into flame.

"There you are," said Rob Roy, pointing to a pile of dried pieces of resinous fir. "Now we can see what we are doing."

Alan looked pale under the ruddy glare of the torch, but the brave little fellow had kept his courage up wonderfully.

In a moment Rob Roy unbound him, and lifting him shoulder high followed Alastair, who carried the torch.

Arrived at the stone steps of the

entrance they soon discovered that it was impossible to move the huge stone from below. Try as they might it would not budge. Rob Roy exerted all his giant strength but the stone was immovable.

"I believe," said Alastair, "that this is but an entrance. The exit must be elsewhere."

"I think you are right," answered Rob Roy. "The stone merely cants to a certain angle on its base, but cannot be moved from below."

"We must try the other way," said Alastair, leading with the torch.

"Lead on," said Rob Roy, lifting Alan on his shoulder.

"You will have to go through the waterfall this way," said Alan.

As they proceeded the cavern opened out into large proportions. It was a weird scene as the dripping water glistened on every side and huge blind bats flapped wildly round the explorers.

"Be careful," said Alastair, warningly, "I hear running water."

As they advanced the sound of the running water became more and more pronounced, and soon they espied a glimmer of light.

Over the slippery rocks they went until the noise of the water surged in their ears.

"The Waterfall of Ard!" shouted Rob Roy.

Alastair nodded his head.

"By all that is wonderful!" exclaimed Rob Roy, as he examined the place carefully. "We are under the waterfall."

Meantime Alan had been trying to attract Rob Roy's attention.

"You will have to step through it to get out!" he kept shouting, trying to drown the noise of the tumbling waters.

"What is that you say?" shouted Rob Roy.

"Step through the waterfall on to the big stone, and then on to the bank."

Midst the rushing mass of water Rob Roy espied a large flat stone.

"That is it," said Alan.

Rob Roy required no further bidding, and stepping through the natural shower-bath stood once more in the open air. With a spring he landed on the mountain side. Alastair followed.

"As your father said, Alan, 'Live and learn.' I have heard of this passage, and now I know it."

CHAPTER XII.

THE ATTACK ON THE STRONGHOLD.

Early next morning the fiery cross was sent round the MacGregor clan, and out of the hundreds of armed clansmen that assembled at the meeting-place on the Braes of Balquhidder fifty were chosen.

The journey was a dangerous one. The appearance of so many MacGregors at one time in the lowlands would have raised suspicions, so it was arranged that the party should make for Galloway in twos and threes, avoiding all the towns *en route.*

They were armed to the teeth—with claymore, dirk, bull-hide targe, pistols and skenedhus.

Rob Roy and Alastair set out first and at the end of three days arrived in the vicinity of the stronghold of the Black Captain.

That night Rob Roy marshalled his clansmen on the bleak moor, and ordering them to take what rest they could, told them that the attack would take place at daybreak.

Wrapping themselves in their plaids the MacGregors lay down to rest, and were aroused at daybreak by the clan pipers playing the "MacGregors Gathering."

"Advance!" cried Rob Roy. "Advance, MacGregors. Follow and spare not!"

"Alastair," said Rob Roy, as they passed the burned-down hut, "see if there are any signs of life about that place."

Alastair ran out to the hut, and soon returned with the answer that the ruins were much the same as they left it.

When they gained the crest of the rising ground that encircled the stronghold Rob Roy ordered the pipers to sound the challenge.

This the pipers did, much to the surprise of the Black Captain and his men as they looked over their castle wall.

Advancing to the moat, where the drawbridge had been raised, Rob Roy shouted:

"You black villain, commonly known as the Black Captain, I call on you to surrender!"

A mocking laugh and a volley of stones was the only answer.

"Fire at the embrasures," ordered Rob Roy.

The MacGregors fired while the robbers dodged behind the walls.

"Assaulting archers to the front!" ordered Rob Roy.

Some fifteen stalwart Highlanders, armed with long bows in addition to their other arms, stepped to the front. Their function was soon apparent, for as they stood in line they affixed burning tow to the end of their arrows, and fired incessant volleys at the raised drawbridge and gateway.

"Keep at it, men; keep at it," shouted Rob Roy, as the burning arrows began to take effect on the woodwork.

The robbers saw their danger as the smoke of the burning gateway began to ascend, and attempted to throw water on it from above, but as soon as a robber showed his face a volley from the MacGregors' pistols drove them back.

Meanwhile the fire took a firm hold of the drawbridge and soon it fell from its hinges a burning mass into the moat.

"Forward!" shouted Rob Roy, waving his claymore as he rushed over the fallen drawbridge and attacked the burning door.

"Make way for the battering-ram," he shouted.

Six powerful MacGregors, holding a fallen tree, rushed at the doorway, which crashed inwards under the impact.

"Follow and spare not! Follow and spare not! Ard Choile! Ard Choile!" shouted Rob Roy, as the MacGregors rushed inside the castle.

With one sweep Rob Roy struck the nearest robber to the ground, while Alastair brought down another.

"Hither you coward, hither you scoundrel!" roared Rob Roy to the Black Captain. "Come hither, and measure swords with me."

But the Black Captain had no desire to meet the valiant chieftain in mortal combat.

"To the keep! To the keep," shouted the Black Captain.

Rob Roy strained every nerve to get near his enemy, but so many of the robbers stood in the way that he found the attempt impossible.

Already the MacGregors were swarming over the castle.

"To the keep! to the keep," again shouted the Black Captain, precipitately retiring.

The keep, the kernel of the strong-hold, stood in the middle of the court-yard, a most unusual place.

"Bring up the battering-ram," shouted Rob Roy.

Instantly the stalwart bearers of the battering-ram rushed at the door of the keep and shivered it in fragments.

Rob Roy sprang through the breach, claymore in hand, but not a soul could he see. The robbers had fled, and in their haste had left the entrance to the secret passage exposed to view.

"Alastair," shouted Rob Roy, "take twenty men and repair with all haste to the burned-down hut. I am certain the exit of the secret passage is there."

But long before Alastair had reached that spot the Black Captain and his followers mounted on fleet horses were beyond the reach of the pursuers.

"Clansmen," said Rob Roy, "you have done well. This night we shall sleep within these walls, and in the morning we shall demolish them."

In the following morning the castle was thoroughly explored, and in one room a large amount of money and valuables were discovered.

"This will be a Godsend to the widows and the poor," said Rob Roy. "Alastair, see that it is all well packed. There will be joy in the Highlands in a few days."

The gold and valuables were packed, and strapped on the backs of sumpter horses, while the secret passage was demolished, and not one stone of the castle left standing on another.

To effect this Roy Roy had ordered his men to pick out the foundation-stones along the walls, while they were propped up with stout wooden props. To these props ropes were attached and at a signal from Rob Roy the powerful MacGregors gave a heave, and down came the castle, a mass of ruins.

"Now for the north," ordered Rob Roy. "Alastair, find a guard for the treasure."

When Rob Roy returned to the Braes of Balquhidder there were scenes of rejoicing.

Ordering all the poor of the clan and all the poor of the tenants of neighbouring lands to be present on a certain day he distributed the money and valuables taken from the robbers' stronghold, thus ensuring those able to work a means of living for a long time to come. As to himself and his picked warriors of the clan, not one cent did they receive. They were proud in their strength, and sufficient it was to them to know that they had a strong right arm, and a sharp, double-edged claymore.

CHAPTER XIII.

THE ROBBER'S CAVE.

But the Black Captain had yet to be reckoned with. He was still at large, and it was yet unknown where he had fled to, whether he had taken refuge amongst the Cheviot Hills, or whether he had made once more for the Highlands, and taken up his abode either in the wilds of Assynt or in the solitudes of Glen Alniac under the shadow of Ben Avon.

When Rob Roy had gained access to the Keep in the Galloway stronghold, the Black Captain gave the order to his men to escape. Running down the secret passage they came to a large underground stable, and mounted without delay, gaining the open air at a place not far from the ruined hut, which in turn was connected with the secret way.

"My men," he said, "ride hard. We shall make for our stronghold in the wilds of Alniac, and once clear of the lowlands we shall pick up what we can by the way."

A couple of days saw them safely through Renfrew and Dumbarton, and another couple of days saw them plodding by the sides of the Cairngorms.

Traversing Glen Avon they arrived at the Alniac—a rattling, roaring mountain torrent, flanked on both sides by precipitous mountains and precipices.

"To-morrow, Johnson," said the Black Captain, "you will take these horses to the fair at Tomintoul and sell them for what they will fetch. They are useless in a country like this. We shall keep the saddles and bridles in our cave."

"And," said Johnson, "if I can find out the buyers we shall be able to lift the horses whenever there is a necessity for it."

"Good man," laughed the Black Captain. "Good man, to-day we shall tether them out under the shelter of the cliffs."

"Dismount," ordered the Black Captain.

Instantly the bandits dismounted, and driving a peg into the ground fastened their horses to them by the head ropes.

"Now to our retreat," said the Black Captain, leading the way.

Going to the edge of the precipice that flanked the roaring Alniac, the Black Captain disappeared from view in an instant. He had apparently leaped over the precipice. But he did no such thing. He merely jumped to a ledge a few yards below, and scrambling on the tree that grew horizontally from the rocks, again dropped to a still lower ledge.

Custom had made them callous, but a false step would have hurled them to death some hundreds of feet in the stream below.

The Black Captain, when he reached the second ledge turned to the right, and, spreading his arms along the rocks as if embracing them, moved cautiously along a narrow goat-track that hung in mid-air. A few yards brought him to firmer ground and to a ledge that at the first glance showed the entrance to a cavern.

"Now then, my men," said the Black Captain, when the last man had crossed the narrow goat-track, "we can defy capture. Woe be to the man that attempts to cross that dizzy height. Let us rest in the meantime."

The men entered a huge cavern on the floor of which were beds of dry, sweet-smelling heather. Several boxes lay about, while the walls were decorated with numerous swords and knives. This was one of the northern retreats of the Black Captain to which he retired when hard pressed and from which he could sally out at leisure.

Taking a draught of cool water from a limpid spring that bubbled in a corner of the cave, the Black Captain flung himself on his bed of heather.

On the following day the horses were unsaddled and the saddles let down by ropes to the cavern's mouth and stowed away for future use.

"Well, Johnson," said the Black Captain, when his henchmen returned from Tomintoul after disposing of the horses, "did you see any one you knew?"

"That I did not," replied the man, jocularly, "except this old friend." And he produced two huge flagons of whisky. I got a farmer to give me a lift as far as the Avon."

The Black Captain smiled.

" To-night we shall cast about for provisions."

That night they did, and created havoc all over the neighbourhood. From the first farm they came across they seized a horse and cart, entered the house, stole all the cheese, butter, eggs, and bread that they could, insulted the inhabitants, packed their spoil in the cart, and drove off.

They visited the various farms and stole what they could. They wrung the necks of as many fowls as they fancied they could use, stole a fat lamb or two, and retired with their spoil.

" Now, my men, for home," laughed the Black Captain. When they had lowered the spoil to the cavern they unyoked the horse, deliberately turned it adrift, and wantonly ran the cart over the precipice, where, amidst their jeers and laughter, it was smashed to atoms on the rocks below.

The wretched inhabitants soon became aware that the evil Black Captain was again in their midst, and in their terror one name came prominently before them. That was the name of the great Highland outlaw chieftain, Rob Roy—outlawed simply by the caprice of the Government at the instigation of his private enemies.

When things were at their worst, Hamish McDuim, a daring young Highlander, was deputed to ask the help of Rob Roy, and in a couple of days Hamish was laying the case of the crofters of Glen Avon before the noble chieftain.

" And you say," said Rob Roy to Hamish, " that the Black Captain has a retreat by the banks of the Alniac. 'Tis a wild spot and I know it well."

" It is said," returned Hamish, " that the Black Captain inhabits a cavern, but no one knows for certain, because it is certain death to go within a mile of the place. But certain it is that they have a holding of some kind there, and they live well."

Rob Roy thought deeply.

" It is useless until we know exactly how the land lies to attack in force. There is only one thing for it. I was looking forward to a few days' rest, but never let it be said that the MacGregor turned a deaf ear to an appeal for help. Tell your people that I will

succour them, and that if I cannot capture or kill the Black Captain I shall drive him from your lands."

Hamish departed for home in high glee.

Meanwhile, Rob Roy had made up his mind. There was only one thing for it, and that was to beard the robbers in their den in disguise. This was a most daring thing to do for many of them to their cost knew Rob Roy, and with his giant frame and sparkling eyes disguise was almost impossible.

However, he determined to track the robbers down.

Donning the Gordon tartan he set out for the far north, and in the disguise of a cattle drover from Donside he put up at the village of Tomintoul.

As he mixed with the farmers at the fair and discussed the price of cattle he came face to face with Johnson, his erstwhile jailor in the Galloway stronghold.

Johnston started back, and Rob Roy, to put him off the scent at once tackled him.

" Good morning to you, fair sir, and have ye any spare stirks wi' ye ? "

" Aye that I have, but they are all sold," replied Johnson.

" Ah," returned Rob Roy, " and that is a peety, for I've taken a fancy to ye and like dealing wi' honest men. At any rate, ye'll hae a quaich ? "

" Wi' pleasure," responded Johnson, eyeing Rob Roy keenly, " lat's to the booth."

They both adjourned to the drinking booth in front of the hotel, where Rob Roy ordered two jorums of uisgebae, or in plain English, two large glasses of whisky.

" Your health," said Rob Roy, sipping out of both glasses (according to the old Highland custom, to show that there was no poison in the mead) before handing the quaich to Johnson ; " your health, sir."

" Your very good health. Slaunch ! "

Rob Roy made a great display of his purse and money when he paid for the whisky, so much so that Johnson was compelled to make comment.

" You seem to have a purse well lined, sir," said Johnson.

" Oh, nothing to what I have at home," replied Rob Roy. " You see, I am the owner of three farms, an' they are well stocked."

" And where might that be, if I may be so bold ? "

"In the Cabrach," replied Rob Roy.

"I don't know it, but I have heard it is a very fine district."

"It is. A very fine district," chuckled Rob Roy; "but have another quaich. No, no, I'll take no refusal. Donald, another two."

Rob Roy took a long draught and pretended that the whisky was taking effect on him.

"A very fine district, indeed," he continued. "In fact, I do very well there. I said three farms, but, believe me, I might have said thirty."

Johnson seemed nonplussed.

"I have seen you before somewhere," he said.

"That might be. I often come here to the fairs, particularly when there's cattle about."

"To buy?" asked Johnson.

Roy Roy gave a hoarse chuckle.

"No, no, my man; to sell, sir, to sell. Do you understand?"

"We're at the same game," said Johnson, looking Rob Roy straight between the eyes.

"Your hand, my man," said Rob Roy, feigning great confidence; "your hand, my man. Listen," he added, as if the whiskey had taken possession of his brain. "Listen, I'm a cattle lifter. Thirty farms. Three hundred farms. D'ye see?"

Johnson bent forward, and shook hands as Rob Roy whispered in his ear, "A fine country the Cabrach."

"Is it any use giving you a hand," asked Johnson.

"Well," returned Rob Roy, with assumed gravity, "well, no. It is a fine country, but I prefer to do my own."

"But with help you could do a roaring trade."

"True, but though I like your face, and trust you, you must confess that to take a stranger in partnership might be a wrong move. Where's your place?"

"Not far from here. Up the Alniac."

"Up the glen that is."

"Yes. I'm ready for a bargain."

"Well, mine is a very good trade, and I should like to see some proofs of your substantiality."

"That you can do to-day—now."

"I cannot come wi' you now," replied Rob Roy, "but to-morrow I can make an appointment. Give me the directions."

"Ye cross the Avon below the village, and follow the bridle-path by the Alniac where it runs into the Avon. For two miles keep by the path, and I will meet you there."

"Are you alone?"

"Well, no! To tell you the truth I am the leader of a band twenty-two strong."

"He is telling the truth for once—or partly so," thought Rob Roy. "Twenty-two strong," added Rob Roy, loudly; "a big force."

"Fairly so; but meet me to-morrow, and then we can go into details. We could do some fine lifting in the Cabrach."

"I have no doubt you could," thought Rob Roy.

"To-morrow then at what time?"

"Oh!" replied Rob Roy, "say twelve midday. I have some business to transact in the morning."

"So let it be. Then good-bye in the meantime."

"Good-bye," replied Rob Roy, thickly pretending to stagger to his feet. "Good-bye. To-morrow at twelve."

Johnson left the booth, and when he was out of sight Rob Roy quickly entered the hotel where he thought out his plans.

"He suspected me from the first," muttered Rob Roy, "but I think I have convinced him. However, to make certain I shall not meet him, but to-night before the sun goes down I shall track him to his lair."

Rob Roy now laid aside his kilt, and dressed himself in tartan trews like a Highland shepherd engaged in sheep-shearing, at the same time concealing a pair of carefully loaded pistols in his plaid, together with a couple of sharp dirks.

All that afternoon from the window of the hotel in the market square he watched the throng, and particularly the Black Captain's henchman who from repeated libations at the booth was becoming rather unsteady on his feet.

At last Roy Roy saw him depart from the village, and take his way towards the Avon.

Crossing the ford just above where the Alniac joins the Avon, Johnson struck the bridle-path, and Rob Roy followed at a judicious distance.

Unaware that he was being followed Johnson trudged along for a considerable distance, and suddenly disappeared.

"I know the trick," said Rob Roy, 'and near this spot I take up my abode for the night."

The tops of the precipitous cliffs were covered with heather and giant bushes of yellow broom, and under one of the latter he found sufficient cover.

Scarcely had he concealed himself than the familiar figure of the Black Captain approached and disappeared over the brink of the precipice.

"I shall see what I can do for you, my esteemed friend," thought Rob Roy.

In a little while another of the robbers approached and disappeared at the same spot.

Darkness now closed in, and Rob Roy settled himself for the night. It was a long, weary wait, but daylight came at last, and with it appeared the gang of freebooters.

One by one they appeared over the edge of the precipice, and were marshalled by the Black Captain not five yards from Rob Roy's place of concealment.

The Highland Chieftain dared scarcely breathe.

"What would they not give to know I was here," thought our hero.

"Twenty-two all told," thundered the Black Captain. "To-day we pay visits to the farms of Wilarmore, and Campdale. They purchased most of the cattle at yesterday's market, and we must relieve them."

The Black Captain chuckled hoarsely. "Forward, men," he shouted, as he led them away.

Rob Roy breathed more freely, but did not move for some time. Moving his cramped limbs he arose, but took the precaution to have the bush of broom between him and the departing robbers in case any of them should suddenly return.

At length he followed in their track, and from a coign of vantage saw them make for the ford.

Retracing his steps Rob Roy arrived at the spot where he had seen the robbers disappear.

"It is as I thought," he muttered, "an ingenious scheme certainly."

Dropping lightly on the ledge, he slipped on to the tree and balanced himself. Lowering himself carefully to the lower ledge he saw that the only way open was by the goat track.

Like the skilled mountaineer that he was, this treacherous path presented no obstacle to our hero. Embracing the rocks with his outstretched arms he moved cautiously along, and gained the entrance to the cavern.

Rob Roy was struck with admiration. "Why," he exclaimed, "this place is impregnable. One man could defy an army. One push and the attacker is hurled to instant death."

As Rob Roy examined the cavern more minutely, he gave vent to exclamations of surprise, particularly when he discovered that many of the boxes were full of money.

"This will do for my poor," he exclaimed.

Rob Roy examined the roof carefully. The cavern had evidently been extended by human hands, for much of the roof was of sandy soil, and shored up with piles of young fir-trees.

As his eye caught the saddles, swords, and pistols, a thought struck him.

"Now to disarm them, but I must be quick." Retaining a sword for his own use, he dragged everything he could to the edge of the cavern—saddles, swords, blankets, pistols, ammunition, boxes of clothing, &c.—and as quickly as he could hurled them all into the abyss below, even to the feather beds.

In a very short time the cavern was denuded of everything except the boxes of treasure, and no trace was left that any human being had been there during the absence of the robbers. Everything had disappeared as if by magic.

Rob Roy then felt his way along the dizzy goat track, and mounting the tree scrambled on the ledge and thence to firm ground above.

Once more he concealed himself in the bush of broom, until he should think his plans out.

Alone, he was unable to prevent the raid on Urlarmore and Campdale, and rightly judging that a stranger organising help against the Black Captain would only create suspicion, he decided to make for the village before setting out for home.

Keeping a sharp look out he arrived at the village in safety.

"I wonder," he laughed, "what the Black Captain will think of his retreat now?"

What the Black Captain did say cannot be repeated. The villain cursed and swore, stamped and raved, and when his rage had expended itself, he listened to his gang.

With the exception of one man, they all put it down to the work of the evil one, but that one man knew that he was not mistaken in the cattle trader he had met on the previous day.

And he told the Black Captain what he thought.

CHAPTER XIV.

A Hazardous Journey.

It was night when Rob Roy left the village of Tomintoul.

So pitch dark was it that he, accustomed as he was to thread the most dangerous paths at night, even experienced difficulty in travelling quickly.

"Once I am clear of the glen and amongst the hills," thought Rob Roy, "it will be easier travelling; but this dark glen is unsafe. I ought to have taken the high road for it. Even the stars cannot be seen."

Rob Roy plunged onwards through the waving bracken, thick undergrowth, and stumpy trees that bestrewed the rough cart track through the glen.

His only guide was his feet, and when they did not grate on the ground cut up by horses' hoofs, he knew that he was in danger of losing his way.

Suddenly he was flung right on his face. A tingling sensation shot along his shins.

"A wire man-trap," he muttered, as he staggered to his feet.

In a moment he was down again, while he floundered about in the meshes of wire cunningly laid.

A mocking laugh re-echoed through the glen. It was the laugh of the Black Captain.

Rob Roy lay still for a second, while the heavy step of some one approaching was heard close at hand.

But our hero was not dismayed. The wire seemed to encircle him everywhere.

He lay still and deliberately disentangled himself, creeping slowly backwards until he felt he was free from his bonds.

"The great MacGregor," said the mocking voice of the Black Captain, "is once more in the power of the oppressor of the poor, et cetera."

The Black Captain's voice sounded close at hand, but Rob Roy did not respond. He crept backwards in dead silence.

Feeling himself amongst the heather Rob Roy awaited events.

"MacGregor!" exclaimed the Black Captain, sarcastically, "you are quiet for once, but pray tell me how you enjoy the small diversion I invented for your pleasure!"

Rob Roy made no reply. He could only guess the direction of the Black Captain in the darkness. But his mind was made up.

"The friend of the poor," sneered the Black Captain, "has found a comfortable lodging from which he shall not be disturbed till the morning's light."

Rob Roy's silence exasperated the Black Captain.

"Speak, you dog!" he exclaimed fiercely. "Speak! No power on earth can save you!"

Rob Roy, meanwhile, was busily engaged. Quickly and silently he was pulling the thick dry grass and heather in a heap.

An oath escaped from the lips of the Black Captain.

Rob Roy was now satisfied that the heap of grass and fibre in front of him was sufficient.

Thrusting his flint-lock pistol into the heap, he fired. The grass deadened the sound of the discharge, but instantly a flame shot upwards.

The spark from the flint had ignited the grass, the flame travelling like lightning speed towards where the Black Captain's voice had come from.

By the lurid glare Rob Roy, from his place of concealment, saw that the path in front of him was strewn with wire entanglement, taken from the fences of the neighbouring farm of Urlarmore.

"The heather is on fire! The heather is on fire!" shrieked the Black Captain. "Run for your lives, men, run for your lives!"

"Then," muttered Rob Roy, "I have made a providential escape."

As he spoke a score of figures darted from the surrounding bushes and fled for their lives, pursued by the shooting tongues of flame.

In a few moments the glen was like a cauldron.

"I must be quick," muttered Rob Roy, as the fire began to creep near him. "I must move at once, for if the wind changes, I will also be caught."

Starting to his feet he quickly retraced his steps, going in the opposite direction to the Black Captain and his band of robbers.

"I must strike for the high road," said Rob Roy, as he seized the bushes and clambered up the sides of the mountain. "And I must be quick or I shall fall foul of these cut-throats again."

By the light of the blazing valley Rob Roy soon gained the top of the mountain and reached the "high road," or long winding road that led over the mountain's crest. It was the longer road, the glen below being the short cut."

"The longest way is often the quickest," muttered Rob Roy. "Now let me sit a moment and think."

"If I move now I may fall foul of those villains. They have gone to the other end of the glen, and they may have returned by the other side of the river. One thing is certain, they want my blood."

Rob Roy pondered deeply, and at last resolved to proceed on his way.

"Even," he said, "if I wait until daylight, the danger is the same. Besides, it were better that I should cross the lands of the Grahame to-morrow night rather than by day."

Saying so, Rob Roy sprang to his feet, and pursued his journey. As he crossed the top of the mountain and descended the other side, the light from the burning valley lit up the whole of the surrounding country.

"Ha, ha!" laughed a sardonic voice, "there is such a lovely moon to-night that we can discern the check of the red tartan of the Red MacGregor."

It was the Black Captain.

"And you may taste the edge of the claymore of the same," replied Rob Roy testily, as he drew his claymore.

"Resistance is useless," laughed the Black Captain, in a hollow voice.

"By the same token, it is," replied Rob Roy, boldly. "Stand aside and let me pass. I care not though you be backed by all your cut-throats. Stand aside, I say, and let me pass."

"Not while your head is worth £1,000, and not while £5,000 awaits in Edinburgh the man who captures the great hero alive."

"Stand back," shouted Rob Roy, advancing.

The Black Captain laughed and retired for a few yards.

Rob Roy saw the trap. The Black Captain's men were in hiding by the roadside in the hope of catching our hero behind as he followed the arch robber.

Instantly Rob Roy bent down, and, drawing his dirk from the top of his stocking, threw it with unerring aim at the Black Captain.

The Black Captain staggered back, pinned through the shoulder.

"At him, men! At him!" he shouted, ferociously. "At him! Capture him alive if possible. If not, off with his head."

It was well for Rob Roy that he was prepared. From all sides the robbers sprang from the heather and violently attacked our hero, but it was evident that they dreaded his terrible claymore.

Rob Roy sprang at the nearest robber and cut him down with one blow.

"You scoundrel," shouted Rob Roy, at the Black Captain, "you scoundrel. Stand your ground. I follow you not."

But the Black Captain, for some reason or other, kept on retreating.

Suddenly the robbers made a simultaneous rush. Rob Roy plied his double-edged claymore valiantly, making every stroke tell, but it was evident the robbers were determined to capture him this time.

Soon our hero found that he was fighting for his life. Blows rained on him on every side, and it was only by the clever use of his targe in defence and of his claymore in attack, that he held his ground.

Three powerful robbers flung themselves on Rob Roy, two on the left and one on the right. Our hero cut down the latter, while one of the men on the left aimed a terrific blow at Rob Roy's head. Rob Roy caught the blow on his targe, but the third man made a desperate lunge.

Rob Roy sprang forward and ran him through the gullet, while the second man again struck at our hero's undefended head.

Like lightning Rob Roy turned, and with a sliding movement, received the blow on his targe, at the same time striking the man full in the chest with the skenedhu he held concealed in his left hand behind his shield.

But in an instant half a dozen more robbers were round him. It was a fight for life. Right and left Rob Roy struck out, but, strong man that he was, he felt the effect of the onset. The place seemed to be swarming with robbers.

Rob Roy felt himself in a tight corner, and, hero that he was, that fact made him fight more fiercely than ever.

"Yield, MacGregor!" shouted the Black Captain, who had been hovering on the outskirts of the battle. "Yield, MacGregor! Capture him alive, if possible," he shouted, alternately addressing our hero and the robbers.

"Not while I draw breath," returned Rob Roy, laying another robber low. "Come on, you scoundrel."

For answer the Black Captain picked up a stone and hurled with fearful force at Rob Roy's head.

It caught the Highland chieftain on the temple, and though but a glancing blow, struck him to the ground.

In an instant a dozen swords were at Rob Roy's throat.

"Yield or die," hissed the Black Captain.

"Never! Never! Grigalach for ever!"

As if by magic the war-cry was repeated.

"Grigalach for ever! Grigalach for ever!"

The Black Captain stood aghast. The robbers raised their swords in alarm.

Like the rushing wind a body of Highland shepherds, led by Hamish McDuim, all armed with scythe-blades, stuck on the end of poles, crashed in amongst them.

Wielded by brawny arms, these improvised weapons did terrible execution.

"Strike for the noble MacGregor!" thundered Hamish McDuim, almost severing the nearest robber in two with his fearful weapon.

In an instant Rob Roy was on his feet, as the blood trickled from his forehead.

"Follow and spare not! Follow and spare not!" he shouted, rushing after the discomfited robbers.

"That we will," returned Hamish McDuim, grimly, as he cut down still another robber.

But the other robbers did not wait, and the Black Captain was nowhere to be seen.

"Hamish McDuim," said Rob Roy, shaking Hamish by the hand, "I thank you. I hope to do for you what you have done for me."

"What I have done for you, nob... MacGregor!" exclaimed Hamish. "Wh... we have done is but a poor return... what you have done for us. You have ve... tured your life and freedom for our sa... and we give but an earnest of what... shall do in the future. The fire in t... glen woke us up, and we saw at on... how matters stood. I thought y... were not leaving Tomintoul until... morrow."

"I thought it better, good Hamish, act at once," replied Rob Roy, "and... that reason I must proceed at once."

"And we shall accompany you," sa... Hamish McDuim.

"No, no, good Hamish. I can w... take care of myself."

"We know that, noble MacGrego... returned Hamish, "but all the same... shall conduct you by the short cut... Nethy Bridge."

"So be it, Hamish; let us proceed."

Much to Rob Roy's delight, Ham... McDuim showed him some of the n... cuts on his way home.

"Hamish," said Rob Roy, as he par... on the confines of Inverness-shire,... thank you and your good comra... very much. When I return it shall... at the head of the MacGregors, and... case we shall not be able to effect t... capture of the Black Captain and... gang at the outset, I shall not call... you in case vengeance may fall on you...

"I thank you, Rob Roy," repli... Hamish, "but methinks the Bla... Captain will know my face again."

"That he will," laughed Rob R... "and I am sure you can defend yourse... but in the attack on the Black Capt... and his gang I must proceed with cautio... Therefore, Hamish, adieu! Again... thank you and your brave shepher... Some day I may be able to repay yo... To you I owe my life, and I shall n... forget it."

And shaking hands with Hamish a... his comrades, Rob Roy strode away.

The following day saw Rob R... tramping through the lands of t... Grahame, his hereditary enemy.

With a light step and cheerful hea... he bounded over the heather.

When the red tartan of the MacGreg... was seen the greatest excitement pr... vailed in the villages, and a few of t... clan went out in pursuit.

"Hold there, MacGregor! Why tre... pass you in the lands of the Grahame?

"Trespass?" exclaimed Rob Roy indignantly. "Trespass? I know not the word. I plead ignorance. I have not the same opportunity as you for hobnobbing with the lawyers of Edinburgh."

"What mean you?" shouted the leader of the Grahames, in anger. "What mean you?"

"I mean," retorted Rob Roy, "that you and your clan are the hangers on of the Court; that you and your clan are the persecutors of the MacGregor; and that you and your clan are not worthy of the country. Make way! Make way for a true Highlander!"

"Make way? Make way for a MacGregor?" asked the Grahame.

"It is not the first time," retorted Rob Roy, drawing his claymore. "You forget the incident of the eagle's nest. At that time I said my good sword was my passport. Therefore, unless you desire to taste it, make way!"

The Grahames, remembering the time when Rob Roy climbed the face of a precipitous mountain and saved a Grahame baby from the clutches of an eagle, when the Grahames themselves dared not venture to the rescue, fell back.

"Not that I wish to recall that incident," exclaimed Rob Roy, as he strode forward, "but my good sword is my passport."

And so it was until he reached the lands of his clan.

CHAPTER XV.

THE ASSAULT.

When Rob Roy returned home, he mustered the clan, and chose fifty of his best fighters to accompany him to the northern retreat of the Black Captain.

It was a hazardous undertaking, for the MacGregors had to pass through the lands of their mortal enemies the Grahames, and their passage was likely to be disputed.

The Grahames, high in favour at Court, had stooped at nothing in order to bring the MacGregors into disrepute, urging on the Government, for instance, that the deeds of the Black Captain were the doings of the clan. But despite the cruelty of the Grahames, and their cunning and their intriguing, the clan Gregor flourished like a bay-tree.

With thoughts like these in his breast the gallant chief of the MacGregors set out on his self-imposed mission, but before he had been one day on the march the Grahames got wind of it.

Everything that was required for the expedition was paid for, Rob Roy himself giving high and fancy prices to the poor with whom he dealt in preference.

On the second day of the march, several skirmishers of the Grahames were observed, but they contented themselves with keeping at a safe distance.

"MacGregors," said Rob Roy, "keep your eyes open. The Grahames fancy that they are leading us into a trap, but they will get cold steel instead."

It was as he said. On the third day the advance guard of the MacGregors reported the pass in front was swarming with Grahames in ambush.

Rob Roy immediately strode to the front, and in a voice of thunder issued a challenge.

"Ye cowardly Grahames. I challenge any of you to mortal combat. I see you skulking in the heather, but remember you are powerless to stop the advance of the MacGregors."

No answer was given to the challenge.

"Piper," shouted Rob Roy, "sound the slogan."

The piper immediately struck up a stirring tune, while Rob Roy ordered the advance by the right.

The Grahames, trusting to their superior numbers, left their ambush, and prepared to oppose the advance.

"Ard Choile! Ard Choile! Charge MacGregors! Charge!" shouted Rob Roy, springing to the front, and waving his claymore. "Grigalach! Grigalach!"

With a mighty roar the MacGregors dashed on the Grahames. Claymore clashed with claymore and targe, but nothing could withstand the impetuosity of the MacGregors.

"Grigalach! Grigalach!" shouted Rob Roy, encouraging his clansmen, and cleaving a way for them to follow.

Before his terrible claymore the Grahames fell back.

"Back, you cowardly Grahames. Back! and allow the MacGregors on an errand of mercy."

With each word, Rob Roy's sword swept the air, and the quicker he advanced the more precipitate became the rout of the Grahames until they fled in utter confusion.

"So much," said Rob Roy, as he marshalled his clansmen—"so much for the favourites and hangers on at Court. Robbers legalised by Royal favour."

Roy Roy then resumed his march, and kept a sharp look-out in the rearguard in case the Grahames should attack him from behind.

However, they thought better of it, and in a few days the MacGregors arrived in the vicinity of the depredations of the Black Captain.

"Alastair," said Rob Roy, "go to the farm of Urlarmore and explain matters. See if we cannot encamp on their land for a night or two, or for such time as we can lay the Black Captain by the heels."

Alastair went, and was received with open arms when he had explained his mission.

"But I must swear you into the greatest secrecy. If a breath escapes of our presence here, then we have a bootless task."

The farmer promised secrecy.

"It is hardly necessary for me," he said, "to say so, and I should advise you not to move until night. Then under cover of darkness you can reach the banks of the A'an, and following them arrive at the Lower Haugh, where even in the daytime you will be sheltered from all observation."

Alastair thanked him, and withdrew.

That night the MacGregors moved on Urlarmore, and following the directions given, reached the Lower Haugh, where the farmer himself was waiting for them.

There they made themselves comfortable for the night.

"I say, Urlarmore," said Rob Roy, "one word before you go. In the morning I want all the spades and picks you can lay your hands on."

"Spades," said the farmer in surprise.

"Yes, spades," laughed Rob Roy. "I want to dig the cunning old fox from his lair if he won't come by persuasion."

"You shall have them," laughed the farmer, "and good luck to you. Goodnight."

When morning broke the farmer had gathered all the spades and pickaxes of all shapes and sizes he could gather on his own and neighbouring farm and brought them to the Lower Haugh.

"To-day," said Rob Roy, "we sh rest, for by this time the Black Capta may have left, but early next morni we shall pay him a visit."

In the middle of the night the Ma Gregors, armed to the teeth, and carryi spades, set out for the cavern of t Black Captain.

Noiselessly they passed through To intoul, and crossing the ford climb the bridle-path.

Silently Rob Roy placed them alo the edge of the precipice and awaited daylight.

When day broke, Rob Roy could he the robbers moving about.

Placing himself exactly over t ledge that gave access to the cave below, he awaited the appearance the Black Captain.

Soon he was rewarded.

As the Black Captain stepped on t lower ledge, preparatory to negotiati the narrow goat track, his eye cau the giant form of the MacGregor gaz down upon him intently.

With an oath he sprang back.

"It is my turn now, thou evil doer exclaimed Rob Roy, sternly.

The Black Captain gave a mocki laugh.

"Turn, you Highland outlaw. what right do you speak to me?"

"By that right that God gave strong the power to protect the we thou trampler on the poor, thou robl of the widow, thou despoiler of orphan."

"Bah!" exclaimed the Black Capta fiercely. "Bah! I care not for th If I am in thy power, why not come do and turn me out?"

"There are more ways than one, th villain, and I tell thee thy days numbered," and Rob Roy tapped basket hilt of his claymore.

"Why not come down and fight then?" exclaimed the Black Capta his face growing blacker with passio

"I challenge you to mortal comba said Rob Roy, coldly, "I challenge to meet me here, where man to n there is neither fear nor favour."

"And if I refuse?"

"Your blood be upon your o head!"

The Black Captain laughed sardo cally.

Rob Roy MacGregor," he said, " I
n you. I jeer at you. Come down
and put in effect the brave words
use."

Once more I call on you to sur-
er," said Rob Roy, sternly.

Surrender ? Why bandy words and
e time ? I defy you. I defy you."

So be it then," said Rob Roy, and
the signal to Alastair.

stantly thirty picks and spades
led by powerful arms set to work
he ground overhead.

ie thumping of the pickaxes smote
he Black Captain's ears. He turned
ale as death.

Ah!" said Rob Roy. "You blanch,
ou. I said your time has come!"

What mean you ? I understand
not," replied the Black Captain, for
first time in his life showing a trace
motion.

I mean that I shall dig you out,"
Rob Roy, triumphantly. "There
more ways than one in catching a
Some hunt them ; in the High-
s, as you are aware, we shoot them
ermin."

ie Black Captain was evidently
urbed, but he made strenuous efforts
nceal his anxiety. Perhaps, thought
the tough mountain shingle and
her coated ground will resist the
es.

You may do what you like!" he
ted in anger. "We are prepared
ou."

ie ground did indeed prove stubborn,
the MacGregors worked with a will.
The roof of the cavern cannot be
than six feet down," said Alastair.
hen you dig about four feet, stop,
then we shall use a battering-
"

ob Roy kept his eye on the Black
ain, who immediately afterwards
ppeared and entered the cavern.

e gazed at the roof carefully.

Place as many of these planks as
can against the walls," he said to his
. "The fools are trying to dig
ugh, but they will surely dig their
graves."

gain he returned to the ledge.

Yield ye, Black Captain!" shouted
Roy, in salute.

Go, Rob Roy!" returned the Black
ain in scorn. "Go and talk to
lren. Do not bother me."

Your escape is cut off and you might

as well die properly as like a rat in a
hole."

"My choice is my own," sneered the
Black Captain, as he again retreated
into the cavern.

By this time the MacGregors had
dug a large square hole about four feet
deep.

"Be careful!" shouted Alastair.
"Stop digging, and bring up the battering-ram."

The battering-ram was but a large
tree that had been cut down.

"Now, altogether!" shouted Alastair,
as they banged the tree in the excavation.

"Once more. Altogether!"

The ground shook beneath the blows,
but the top of the cavern still resisted.

"Take your spades and picks!"
said Alastair. "Take another foot off,
but be careful."

The MacGregors again set to work with
a will, and in a short space of time dug
deeper down.

"Try the battering-ram again," said
Alastair.

The battering-ram was again brought
forth, and the ground sank beneath its
blows.

"Once again!" shouted Alastair.

The ground was caving in.

"Stand back!" shouted Alastair, as,
with a rumbling noise, the whole roof of
the cavern collapsed, burying alive in
the *debris* the whole band of robbers, save
their leader, the Black Captain,— who
stood aghast on the ledge.

From above the MacGregors gazed
down on the ruins. Only a mass of
earth was to be seen, and not a single
sign of life save the solitary figure at the
cavern's mouth.

"Alastair!" shouted Rob Roy.
"Stand here and prevent the escape of
the arch-fiend until I descend into
the cave and settle with him."

The Black Captain did not hear. He
stood spell-bound.

Sword in hand, Rob Roy leapt into
the cavern.

"Draw and defend yourself!" he
shouted. "Your hour has come. I
will give you five minutes to make your
peace with outraged heaven."

"Bah!" exclaimed the Black Captain,
fiercely. "Cease your prating."

With a curse the Black Captain
sprang forward and thrust at Rob Roy,
who parried the blow.

Both were splendid swordsmen, and

both stood on their guard, playing a waiting game.

Gradually Rob Roy advanced without striking a blow, but pushing the Black Captain nearer and nearer the edge of the precipice.

The Black Captain observed the manœuvre, and in order to defeat it made a thrust at Rob Roy.

The Highland chieftain thrust the blow aside and cut the Black Captain on the face.

With a howl of rage and pain the Black Captain made a mighty stroke at Rob Roy, who deftly struck the blow aside and kept advancing step by step.

There was no escape. Try how he might the Black Captain could not break Rob Roy's guard, and slowly and surely the Highland chieftain was forcing him to his death.

" Murderer, robber, oppressor, your doom is sealed," said Rob Roy, sternly, " and may the Lord have mercy on your soul."

Like lightning the Black Cap thrust at Rob Roy's throat.

The Highland chieftain leapt to side, and with one terrible sweep o double-edged claymore hurled the B Captain over the precipice.

With a howl of despair the B Captain disappeared, and was dashe pieces on the rocks two hundred below.

" The question now," said Rob looking up from the cavern, " is wh we should leave the bodies here b as they are, or whether we sh disturb them for the sake of the treas

" Leave them, Rob Roy ; leave as they are buried. It was so ordai

" What say you, my clansmen ?

" Leave them, chief, leave them. treasure may be gone, and if it were it would bring bad luck to take it the dead."

" So be it," said Rob Roy, takin his bonnet with the eagle's plume. leave them to a Higher Power. L return to the Braes of Balquhidder.'

THE END.

Printed and Published by James Henderson & Sons, at Red Lion House, Red Lion-court, Fleet stree